Frank Rodgers
The Witch's Dog

PUFFIN BOOKS

PUFFIN BOOKS

Published by the Penguin Group
Penguin Books Ltd, 80 Strand, London WC2R 0RL, England
Penguin Putnam Inc., 375 Hudson Street, New York, New York 10014, USA
Penguin Books Australia Ltd, 250 Camberwell Road, Camberwell, Victoria 3124, Australia
Penguin Books Canada Ltd, 10 Alcorn Avenue, Toronto, Ontario, Canada M4V 3B2
Penguin Books India (P) Ltd, 11 Community Centre, Panchsheel Park, New Delhi – 110 017, India
Penguin Books (NZ) Ltd, Cnr Rosedale and Airborne Roads, Albany, Auckland, New Zealand
Penguin Books (South Africa) (Pty) Ltd, 24 Sturdee Avenue, Rosebank 2196, South Africa

Penguin Books Ltd, Registered Offices: 80 Strand, London WC2R 0RL, England

www.penguin.com

First published 1998
9 10 8

Filmset in Times New Roman

Printed in Hong Kong by Midas Printing Ltd

British Library Cataloguing in Publication Data
A CIP catalogue record for this book is available from the British Library

ISBN 0-140-38466-9

Wilf had a dream.
He wanted to be a witch's
dog.

He wanted to fly to the moon . . .

juggle with
the stars . . .

slide on a moonbeam . . .

and do magic.

But when he told his friends about
his dream, they all laughed.

"Witches don't have dogs," Bertie
giggled.

"They have cats . . .

or rats . . .

They have
bats . . .

or toads . . .

or spiders."

Bertie looked fierce. "Why not be like me?" he said. "I'm a guard dog. People are scared of me."

"But I don't want to scare anybody," said Wilf. "I like people."

"Be like me, then," said Streaky.
"I'm a racing dog. Fast as
lightning."

"I'm slow as treacle," said
Wilf.

"So be like me!" cried Harry. "I'm a sledge dog."

Wilf shivered. "Brrrr!" he said. "Too cold for my tootsies."

Wilf's friends smiled as they went
away.

"A witch's dog!" they said. "What a
laugh!"

Wilf was down in the dumps.
He moped along the street with no
wag in his tail.
Outside a house with a
rather odd front door,
he saw a notice.

Wilf looked at it glumly.
"It doesn't say anything
about dogs," he said.

Then he had a brilliant idea.
"I'll go in disguise!" he thought.

"I'm too big to go as a rat . . .

or a bat . . .

or a toad . . .

or a spider . . .

but I'm just the right size to go
disguised as a cat!"

Wilf rushed home. He got out his paints and a papier-mâché lantern he had made at Hallowe'en.

He cut out two eyeholes in the lantern . . .

stuck on
two pointy
ears . . .

and on the front he painted a
cat's face.

He made a long tail out of a
rolled-up scarf . . .

and tied it on.

Then he put on the mask
and looked in the mirror.
"Perfect!" he said. "Or should
I say *purr-fect*!

I'm sure everyone will think I'm
a cat."
Feeling really pleased with his
disguise he rushed off to the
witch's house.

He rang the bell
and Weenie the
Witch came to
the door.

Witch needs
a pet.
Cats, rats,
bats, toads
and spiders
please apply
within

"Oh goody!" cried Weenie.
"A pet at last. A nice cat.
Please come in, pussy."

18

They went into the kitchen but
Wilf couldn't see very well
under his mask and he bumped
into a chair.

Crack!
The mask split in the middle and
fell off.

"Oh!" gasped Weenie.
"You're not a cat.
You're a dog!"

"Yes," said Wilf, "but I want to be a witch's dog."

"Witches don't have dogs," cried Weenie.

"They have cats, or rats, or bats, or toads, or spiders."

Then suddenly she looked sad and a
big tear trickled down her nose.
"What's wrong?" asked Wilf.

"None of them want to be my
pet," she sniffed.
"Why not?" asked Wilf.

"Everyone says I'm not very good at being a witch," said Weenie.

"You see, I keep on falling off my broomstick . . .

. . . and messing up my spells.
I once turned my Auntie Flo
into a gorilla by mistake."

"No!" cried Wilf.

"Yes," said Weenie. "Luckily she liked being a gorilla and went to live in the jungle."

Wilf smiled.

"If you let me be your witch's dog," he said, "I'll help you to be the best witch in the world."

"Do you think you could?" gasped Weenie in delight.

"Why don't we try?" replied Wilf.

"All right," cried
Weenie. "Let's
try flying first."
She fetched her
broomstick.
"Hop on," she said.

Wilf carefully sat on the end.

27

"Here we go!" cried Weenie.
The broomstick gave a little
hop and a jump . . .

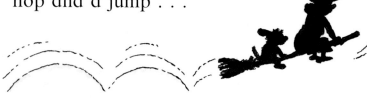

and Weenie fell off.

"Oops!" she said, landing on her
bottom.
The broomstick gave one more hop
and . . .

it shot into the air with
Wilf hanging on tightly.

"Help!" he yelled as the broomstick
turned and twisted
all over the sky.

One minute Wilf was hanging on by
his toes . . .

the next by
his teeth . . .

and the next
by one hand.

The broomstick flew up, down,
sideways and around like a burst
balloon.

WHEEEEEEE

At last Weenie used the proper
magic spell and down it came.

"What you need," said Wilf
dizzily, "are seat belts."

So Weenie went to the car shop
and bought a seat-belt kit. Then
she set to work on her broomstick.

When she had fitted the
seat belts, she took a test
flight. Her first trip wasn't
very good . . .

but she soon got
the hang of it.

"Great!" said Wilf. "Now you won't keep falling off. What's next?"

"My spells always go wrong," said
Weenie.
"Show me," said Wilf.
Weenie opened her big book of
magic.

"Look at this," she said. "I followed
this recipe and instead of becoming
invisible . . .

I became thirty feet tall!
The spell begins . . .
Take one cup of dear soup . . ."

Wilf looked at the book.
"That says *clear* soup, Weenie,
not *dear* soup."

Also in this series...
'Hocus Pocus
for Beginners'

And...

'What's the
Magic Word?'

Spells
and how to
make them

"No wonder my spells always went wrong," groaned Weenie.

"I think you need glasses," said Wilf.

"I think you're right," said Weenie.

So Wilf and
Weenie went
to the optician's.

Weenie tried on lots of pairs of
glasses . . .

and at last she got a pair that were just right.

"Now my spells won't go wrong," she cried. "Hooray! You're a genius, Wilf!"

Outside the optician's, Weenie saw a poster.
"I'm going to read this with my new glasses on," she said proudly.

Pet Show for Witches

Fun, games, magic and competitions

Witches... bring along your pets and enter them in the Grand Witch's Pet of the Year Contest

"Oh!" cried Weenie. "Witch's Pet of the Year! How exciting! Shall we go along, Wilf?"

"Yes, please!" said Wilf.

When Weenie and Wilf arrived
at the show, they saw it was already
full of witches and their pets – cats,
rats, bats, toads and spiders.

Everyone laughed when they saw
Weenie and Wilf.

"A dog can't be a witch's pet!" they
cried.

"Why not?" asked Wilf.

"Just because," they said. "Dogs just aren't right."

"We'll see about that," thought Wilf.

The Pet Competition began.
Wilf trotted proudly beside Weenie
as the witches paraded their pets
round the ring.

"Look, a dog!" said the judges.
"How odd!"

Then the pets did tricks.

Some weren't very good and the
audience groaned.

But everyone cheered when Wilf
balanced an egg on his nose and
juggled six tomatoes in the air at
the same time.

"Hooray!" they yelled.

Lastly the pets did magic.
They were very good at this.
A cat turned into a balloon . . .

A rat became a racing car . . .

A bat turned into a tea-tray . . .

A toad became
a jelly
pudding . . .

and a spider turned
into an octopus.

"Well done!" cried the judges.

"Oh dear," Wilf
whispered. "What
can I do?"
"Try some of my
magic potion,"
said Weenie.

Wilf took some
and began to
grow . . .

until he was bigger than an
elephant . . .

bigger than a house . . .

and even bigger than the tallest
tree.

"Amazing!"
cried
the judges.
"That dog is
the winner!"

Wilf soon came back to his normal size and the judges gave him a medal.

"You are the first dog ever to be Witch's Pet of the Year!" they said. "Congratulations!"

Some of the witches and their
pets were jealous . . .

but everyone else cheered.
"Hooray for Wilf!" they cried.

Wilf's friends were delighted.
"You *are* a witch's dog after all!"
they said. "Well done!"

"Yes. It wasn't such a silly
dream in the end, was it?"
laughed Wilf.

He said goodbye to his friends
and he and Weenie jumped on to
the broomstick. They fastened their
safety belts and . . .

ZOOM! . . . they shot into the sky.

Everyone cheered again.
"Hurray for Weenie the witch!"
they cried. "And for Wilf . . .
the world's first witch's dog!"